for Hamid

Published by John Ott

San Diego, California

cover art by Barbara Sobczyńska

ISBN: 978-1-940830-08-7
Library of Congress Number: 2015902717

JULIA, SKYDAUGHTER

ROBIN WYATT DUNN

CHECKPOINT 473. 6 A.M.

I lost my Daddy in the revolution. My name is Julia. I'm twelve years old. I got my first period last week, the same week of the bombing. There was a lot of blood.

The fighters wear a lot of insignia; some of them corporate sponsors. Some of them symbols of the gods. Me, I wear black. It's a burqa but it's got Batman wings.

My name isn't really Julia; but my Arabic name is a secret.

This story is being posted on the Net, from our ship.

I'm writing it so you know what happened.

So you know what we found.

- -

I remember when my Daddy first told me the story, when he showed me the pictures: *real aliens*, underground. Frozen in time. Their eyes were huge, like dinner plates. Like cybernetic armor in the comic books, shiny and silver and curved.

We'd been digging tunnels for supplies to the Pharaoh (her name is Sarah), but instead our fighters found the Foo fighter.

- -

Today I have to go through the checkpoint. We have a satellite in orbit, did you know that? The trick is to tip it at the right moment...

I am a Factory Worker because I have a good eye, like Andy Warhol. He had a Factory too. But I'm not gay. I like men. But I don't know if they like me...

I don't want to be famous like Andy either. What I want is peace. But Daddy said it's a long way away.

Up ahead are the soldiers with their robots.

If I take my off my burqa when they ask me to, they're going to see the hardware, and I can't let that happen. We can't let that happen. It's not a bomb or anything; bombs are so last century. It's just a little firmware for your systems. Just a little propaganda...

I picked the name Julia because I love Julia Roberts. She has the prettiest smile. I smile when the soldier beckons me forward in the line at the checkpoint. But he can't see it, only my eyes. They're blue.

- -

Blue eyes evolved along with green and grey and amber in Europe, as secondary sexual characteristics.

Big breasts are that way too; designed to distract the eye. To lure the mind. Mine are small. But my eyes are unusual here; they get noticed. They're a distraction. That's what magic is, you know? Watch the birdie fly in the air, while I reach into your wallet...

- -

The Foo fighter was made of a kind of metal alloy we don't know how to make; it reshaped itself after we cut through and then our fighters were afraid they couldn't get back out. Until they learned how to turn the ship on.

Peace is a Wall, but Gates... Gates are something else. One of them I'm going to help build today. With my new software.

- -

I never knew that war could be so beautiful, or that it could hurt this much. A lot of times I want to kill people like you, people who just read about it on the Net. But other times I remember why I'm writing this story. Why we need the explanations to make sense to people like you. People who've never had to live underground.

The checkpoint is a kind of sphincter, an organ in an organism known for its constipation. The scanners are beginning to tune up...

I'm Batman and my Robin flies at 125,000 feet: all I have to do is *chirp* with the transmitter in my hand, and *squeeeeeze:*

RIVER DELTA, WE COPY YOUR LOCATION

is what I hear in my head then.

We can't let the guards know I have transmitters in my skull, or that I have a radio in my hand, or that I have AI software strapped over my breasts.

(And that requires a little prestidigitation, zero to one and one to zero, watch the numbers go round and round and round, like circus clowns...)

The checkpoint has huge metal arms controlled by the soldiers, like the kinds of arms that used to make cars in factories. They swing in and out to scan the people who want in to the city, looking for drugs, neurotoxins, explosive residue, Arabic propaganda, poetry, paintings, encrypted paintings, illegal metals, black market foodstuffs. The scanners find pretty much all of it, unless you tell them to look for something else...

I pray to my god, Bob Kane, inventor of Batman, some crazy white guy in the 20th Century who gave me my awesome wings glued onto the back of my burqa.

My mother is crying right now. As I write this. Sometimes I can even hear her in my sleep. She never wanted me to get the upgrade. Never wanted me to get involved in the revolution. But how are our men supposed to succeed by themselves? We are one flesh.

My mother is forty-five years old. The village said she was too old when she had me, but she wasn't. People say a lot of things that aren't true.

When I went through the checkpoint, my little Satellite Robin sent some ones and zeroes down—what did a little birdie tell you?—well it told me this:

RESET MORNING PROCEDURAL SEARCH
INTERPOLATE POETRY DATA AT
MARK—O! —

The truth is that the soldiers should never have started looking for poetry. I don't know if you know this, but poets have long been killed by kings and emperors here in the Middle East. Poetry's always been political here. It was easy enough, you see, to catch poets when all you had to do was wait for one to start shouting his rhymes in the street, or, God forbid, publish something in a magazine.

But then the government decided they wanted to get ahold of *all* the poetry. Just try writing a software program to recognize what's poetry and what isn't, well, you can try starting with the letter O! —

Ha ha ha!

Those robots will be looking all day.

Meanwhile the corporal waves me through and I bow, and I crush my transmitter into carbon dust in my hand (it hurts a little), and bend under the fallen-tree-trunk-shaped barrier, open the curtain, tighten my veil, and I'm in the city:

PLAZA NINETY-NINE. 6:30 A.M.

I'm not really religious but we have to learn about it in school; it's part of our history. The government tries to pretend it's religious too, mostly with names. They say God has 10,000 names, whatever that means. So this square is the 99th one.

It's beautiful. If I were a princess I'd live here, in one of the levitating self-contained studio apartments overlooking the fountain. It costs about 50,000 credits a month to do that. Which is more than my whole family makes in a year.

But I'm daydreaming. What our fighters have been teaching me is focus: that's my religion now. Focus. Focus. Focus.

Pay attention to everything around me. Everything

and everyone around me is a potential threat. And a potential ally.

Attention, pure and focused attention, is a form of meditation. It's what made the human brain human: meditation. Did you know that? Anyway.

I wipe the carbon dust onto my burqa. That's why I like black; it doesn't show the dirt of the city. (I don't know how the priests can get away with wearing white all the time...)

The aliens are our friends. At least that's what I believe. Even if they're all dead. Even if we never get to meet them in the flesh. They're still our friends; why else would they have left their Gate manual in a language we can manage to read?

"Mango lassi?" asks the brown-skinned boy with the yellow hat, tray balanced in his hand. He smiles at me.

I shouldn't, but they smell really good. Can't little girls have fun once in a while? (Even if she's a revolutionary!) I pass my wrist over the boy's scanner and he winks at me, the little devil.

The mango is like manna in my mouth; I'm walking, I'm walking, up the glass escalator, over the green snapping plants, towards the Emperor's Waterfall, the mango the last treat I'm allowed today, I promise myself... and then I remember the sound of my father's voice, almost like the waterfall ahead, an illusion, rich and full of gravelly stones, and I want to rip off my burqa and throw my firmware into the ghostly water—but I take a deep breath...

The city is like a temple. Full of people. Full of rules. Too beautiful to know what to do with it. Noisy and quiet, noisy and quiet, in waves.

My first mission is to rendezvous with Mr. Ahluwalia. To get my portrait painted.

It was just a trinary language is all, the software on the UFO, which makes sense, since we live in three dimensions. And now our alien friends, wherever they are, are going to help me make a little ID card...

BAZAAR KACHUKHET. 6:45 A.M.

My phone is ringing. Goddamn it, I thought it turned it off. I'm attracting too much attention...

I step under an archway and try to look normal.

"Yes?" I say into the phone at my lip.

"Who is this?" The voice is low and scratchy, like it's compressed. Already it's a security risk.

"Ali-Baba Masseurs at your service!" I say brightly.

"What?"

"We loosen your back and then loosen your purse, bubby!" I whisper, and then hang up. Shouldn't have done that, though. I turn off my phone. I wasn't supposed to be contacted until after 10:30am; that could have been anyone.

I take a deep breath and wade deeper into the bazaar; already it's getting hot. It's been a long summer.

My code name is River Delta. Which is appropriate, since I'm a woman now. And all women are deltas between their thighs...

The carpets and the 3-D water projections hover over the bazaar like genies. I can smell the cardamom and myrrh. Pepper and fried fat. Sweat and camels. Metal and metal and metal. The smithy is down below, but what I need is Painter's Alley. Here my blue eyes attract less notice: bazaars take all comers.

I walk faster, hands on my burqa like a skirt, skipping around the watersellers.

A muezzin is crying the prayers of morning but no one pays attention except a lone dervish, spinning in the nude—I avert my eyes. The Sufis can do anything they want (except own city property...)

It's darker in Painter's Alley. I can smell the oil.

Did I tell you I have red hair, like Julia Roberts too? (I dyed it, my mother flipped out). But I've cut it short. Like a boy. Not that anyone can tell under my burqa.

The burqa is annoying but it is a metaphor appropriate to the revolution: as my body shall soon be unveiled, so shall the Gate. When our worlds join. When the city opens...

"Are you here for a portrait?" asks the salesman at the alley entrance, smiling under his curly moustache.

"Yes, I have an appointment with the journeyman!" I say brightly.

He frowns. This means he will not get an official commission. I move over and stand near him for a moment, closer than is appropriate. In my hand I hold a coin. His hand closes over mine and I feel the thrill of being touched by a man...

I say nothing and walk down into the darker end

of Painter's Alley.

"A customer for you, journeyman!" shouts the mustachioed fellow with the touchy hands.

The Journeyman Painter, younger than I would have guessed, pokes his head out from his curtain, which is a rich and lustrous blue, like the sky. Within is only candlelight.

"Please," he says, bowing.

I bow too, and step inside.

THE PAINTER'S WORKSHOP.

7:05 A.M.

As we resemble God, so do our hands work to make his resemblances near to us. Even as the City nears my heart, with every tick of my little software bomb...

The Painter activates his de-scanner, holding a small black box over his head. It's a noise generator and hunter-seeker algorithm which will prevent government oversight of this position for a period of time, usually sixty minutes. I avert my eyes from its piercing blue light, the same color as his door curtain.

"Now the Emperor is far away," says the Painter.

"You are very young for a journeyman," I say.

"Please make yourself comfortable."

I sit on the pillow provided and remove the headgear of my burqa. Amongst the men of my village, my face is well known, and I rarely veil myself there. But now I feel the thrill of revealing my face to a stranger.

To an artist. My ancestors would be scandalized.

"You are very beautiful," he murmurs, and kneels behind his canvas.

Painters in days of old, both religious and secular, have often been fond of secret messages in their work. The Christians had their allegorical symbols, the Rosicrucians their apocalyptic poems hidden under the oils... our revolution's tradition is not so different.

With the right paintbrush, a painting can be software. Then all you have to do is carry it through the right door...

The nanobots inside his bristles choose which atoms in the oils to encode as our security program, while the Journeyman selects his colors.

"Your eyes are so blue!" he whispers.

I say nothing. I am thinking of my father again, but I must not cry. It would ruin the painting.

Outside in the alley I hear a well-fed child crying for his mother. Just lonely and ornery; I probably woke him up. In my mind, I let his cries be mine. I let his stomach be the stomach of my people. Soon we will all be well fed. Isn't that what all the avatars promised? Moses, Jesus, Mohammed, Batman? Enough food for everyone...

(And a ticket to the stars)

The Journeyman works feverishly, and just to be naughty, I watch his face, and imagine what he might be like in bed.

All religions are aspects of the same truth, of course. The trick is picking which part you need when...

(Even as a drug crosses the blood-brain barrier, the

mandala crosses the boundary between regions of the universe...)

A *mandala* is somewhat dangerous of course. And up to now we've used it only in controlled conditions. But with the aliens' technology we believe we can dismantle huge segments of the surveillance systems that interpenetrate the city...

But I forget that you know nothing. Much of this must be incomprehensible to you. You have forgotten how hard people work to manipulate you. That your Free States are asleep, in so many ways...

I may only be twelve but I am older than you. I have seen men die. I have seen an alien ship. I am fighting a revolution.

"The painting will only be good for the next three hours," says the Journeyman.

I stand and kiss him on the cheek and he smiles.

"The True City thanks you," I tell him. I take the painting and put on my hood and go out under the bright blue canopy.

The people are all around; it is a good market day. Robots spin in the air. Soldiers shuffle with their guns. I strap the painting to my back and people watch; it is possible I am some third or fourth wife, sent to a rich man's harem. Who are they to know?

I lift my skirts again and sprint. I may be a woman but I'm still twelve; I'm allowed.

The lights shimmer over the soul like water. I feel like laughing; like crying. But the burqa hides all but my eyes. They are flint.

PLAZA NINETY-NINE. 8:00 A.M.

I'm running. With two kilos of military-grade firmware carbon strapped to my chest. The City is more beautiful than anything else I have ever seen. More beautiful than the UFO. More beautiful even (though this is sacrilege) than my father's face.

The True City is the City's shadow, held within. The ideal.

I slow to a proper walk befitting a woman of my station (whatever that is). We are supposedly all equal, but that's lost in translation...

Above in the minaret the *muezzin* calls another prayer, which few obey. His voice is like a wild bird. The stones beneath my feet seem to eat me up, burnt sienna, ochre, octagon after octagon... I hold my head up straight. The encrypted painting is strapped to my back. As far as anyone knows I'm just a little ignorant bride-to-be of an off-continent plutocrat.

"What's that you've got there, mademoiselle?" asks an officer. Damn, I didn't see him. The flowers affixed to his vest identify him as a lieutenant. I bow.

"Blessings on you this day, lieutenant."

"Stand up straight and look me in the eye, woman," he says. I do as he says. His eyes are hazel, with a thin marking of chrome around the iris: body scanners.

It could all be over, already. My village... but I can't think about that right now. You're a woman, Julia, use your charms!

I step closer to him and speak in what I think is a sexy voice:

"Would you like me to remove my veil, lieutenant?"

He looks around, nervous suddenly. Good. He's not following a specific order then. He hasn't activated his scanning program.

"It's my last day of freedom, lieutenant! Wouldn't you like a kiss! My betrothed won't mind, he's a liberal!"

"Okay, move along, move along."

I step even closer to him and stare in his eyes, then swirl my veil over his face giving him a glimpse of my cheek, and he gasps, and I run, skirt in my hand, revolution on my back, my heart beating, *thump thump thump*, so loud I bet the satellite can hear it.

(Wait for my signal, Robin... we've got a few hours yet...)

My Batman wings tremble in the hot breeze. Shimmers hover on the horizon over the minarets. The watersellers' cries are like balloons, floating up and up... I buy a draught with my wrist and inhale the cool cold water.

"Merci."

"Goodbye, beautiful," says the old man. I look at his beautiful old face. Then I keep moving.

Ahead is the arch to Plaza Ninety-Eight, and beyond it the Canals.

Some of my people love The City so much they would destroy it rather than see it remain in the hands of tyrants. I cannot agree, though I'm working as hard as any of them to free it. The City is its own being, its own desire, like a wild animal, it's beyond politics in many ways—

Plaza Ninety-Eight is not as accustomed to the burqa. I will have to observe the protocols; move more carefully. I can't retransmit to Robin in orbit for two hours at least... the last burst should still hold though. Nothing to do but find out:

I step in to the queue. Here on the outskirts of The City, all neighborhoods are quarantined. Everyone is watched. Even little girls.

"But I bought it for a song! What do you mean it isn't working!" Two men are arguing over a little robot that follows one of them. It looks like a bewildered Donald Duck, its polish starting to fade.

A woman prays in front of me. An old Achaemenid prayer, to the sun and his cousins. Still the same hot sun, whatever the century...

I shuffle along in line, holding my head up straight.

Everyone around me is like a poem. If I survive... if I make the Gate... I will write a poem. I will recite it in the street. I promise, Father! I promise!

"Step up, step up," says the soldier, barely looking at me. He waves his scanner over me.

Then he waves me through the arch. I'm through.

PLAZA NINETY-EIGHT. 8:15 A.M.

Standing at the level of my shoulder an annoying boy is following me. He can't be more than eight. But he's a pushy little brat.

"Princess! Princess! Invest in my family's shareware program won't you? Only twenty credits, good return!"

"If it's shareware it's supposed to be free, boy," I hiss at him. I'm looking for my canal driver. He's supposed to have a red beard. But this plaza is crawling with beards.

"Nothing is free in this life, Princess! Fifteen credits! Supreme ROI!"

"Beat it!" But some children you cannot get rid of.

"Please, allow me to hold your valuable cargo! Present it to your prince! I will be your slave for the afternoon! Treat you in style!"

"I said, *beat it!*"

"Come, Princess! Please. Have pity on a poor boy like me." The little bastard has the nerve to stick out his lower lip, pouting. He has a handsome face.

"I am no Princess. My name is Julia. What is your name?"

"Julia! My name is Hamid!"

"If you really want to help look for a man in a red beard. I'm meeting a friend of the family."

"You mean like his?"

Hamid points and I see Red Beard, at the other side of a crowd. I dash across the blue diamond-shaped stones of Plaza Ninety-Eight before I remember my manners. I'm in foreign territory now. Step ladylike, Julia, if you don't want to end up with your head in a cryogenic freeze...

(awaiting the Resurrection...)

"Mr. Red Beard, I'm Julia."

He eyes me.

"This is my servant, Hamid. Do you have your boat ready?"

His beard is lustrous, glinting in the light. His eyes are deep set, almost hidden.

"This way," he says. I follow, as is my nature. I slip Hamid a coin, and he cackles like a bird.

THE CANALS. 8:30 A.M.

Constructed much earlier in the Empire's history, they were an homage to Amsterdam, and its mighty trade routes and markets. Though we are no Amsterdam.

Some say our canals are even more beautiful, though. Some still have gold cloth draped over them, so when you row beneath, the sun is ten thousand suns, shimmering all around you.

Hamid is talking, talking, talking. I watch Red Beard's face. My implant transmits some background chatter that I have turned down low; I'm not the only agent in the field today, I know.

We pass a huge man in green robes, like a surly Buddha, delicately balanced in a catamaran, with his four servants rowing as hard as they can. He leers at us as we pass.

I wonder if Red Beard is religious. I dare not ask. If he tries to touch me I'll kick him in the balls.

The water leads us towards the center of The City.

Towards the Emperor's old palace, now unoccupied.

"So you are to be a harem girl, Julia! I knew it!"

"Yes..." I say, playing my part.

"Remember me when you get the Emperor's ear, eh?"

"How could I forget you?"

More boats now. Getting crowded. We row single file, slowly. Entering a tunnel. The darkness is romantic; I hold Hamid's hand, partly out of fear. Red Beard keeps our steady pace, still silent. Hamid is quiet now too. If I die today, at least I will have made a friend.

"Stand single file..." I hear the voice up ahead, at the shadowed docks. This checkpoint will be more dangerous.

It makes sense for me to be an offering to the Secret Emperor. In our paranoid society, being a harem-girl is one of the few things you don't need proper paperwork to do. No girl would make the journey, people think, unless her family had already been paid. And once you go in, you don't go out.

From out of my pocket I take the red rose and ask Hamid to pin it to my burqa. His eyes are dark and sad. Now there will be no doubt about it. I am a present.

"Stand out of the boat..."

Hamid and I get out. I look back at Red Beard. He is already turning round, towards the return canal. I catch his eyes; there is some kind of promise in them. But of what?

This guard is better educated, better dressed. He has the imperial accent. His white trousers look majestic in the reflections of the water, yellow, orange, black, red, white, shifting back and forth. Behind him is a kind of Gate. Not unlike the one we want to bring.

"Stand single file..." I move Hamid in front of me, and put my hands on his shoulders. I feel him tremble. I lean down to whisper in his ear: "You are my servant. You are to be a eunuch." He draws breath. "Don't worry. I only need you for another ten minutes. Is it worth two gold coins to you?" He nods slowly. I stand up straight, watching the guard. He's younger than I thought. From a distance his arrogance made him seem older.

Oh, my Batman wings! How could I forget them. I can no longer be a child, not here. I lean back down and whisper quick: "A present for you Hamid. Take off my Batman wings. They're yours to keep. Give them to your sister. Or wear them yourself."

Hamid solemnly does as he is told, unclipping my wings. He slips them in to his sack.

"They'll be good to you," I say. Then the guard is in front of my face.

"A present for someone, eh?" he says. His voice is higher pitched up close. His eyes look evil to me.

I nod. I say nothing.

"I am the present's servant, sir!" announces Hamid.

The guard says nothing.

"How old are you?" asks the guard.

"She is fourteen sir!" says Hamid.

God bless my little Hamid. I don't trust my own voice. Some battle of emotions is played out over the guard's face; he snarls.

"Go through, go through," he says.

Victory is closer—

THE GATE TO THE INNER CITY.

9:00 A.M.

Time does not work the same in Gates, not once you are inside. They can make you forget. They can make you remember. I haven't been through one since I was five, when we first moved to The City.

I stand behind Hamid, his hand in mine; he's shorter than I am. Over his head I see the tall arc of the Gate, shimmering yellow and white. Through it, as through clear water, I can see the Inner City.

Hamid's dark young skin reflects the yellow light; our hairs begin to stand on end. Then it is our turn. For no reason I can explain, I turn then, looking back, and see the young noble guard look at me, the sneer still on his face, another promise in his eyes.

Perhaps, whatever happens, I will be a possession now. Possessed by The City itself.

We step inside the Gate.

- -

I hear machinery. Like bolts, or robot arms, clanking in a wide and hollow space beneath the earth. What I see is stars, and hills. I see dead temples. Still I feel Hamid's hand.

I see a long line of baby robots, no taller than my knee, arranged in a long line; I know they are awake. (Perhaps these are the harem girls...)

What I know now is that the Gates were not made by the Emperor's men. They are like the UFO my people found: alien technology. My father explained to me as a girl, and I explain to you now, whoever you are: the Gates can let you travel very far, just by stepping through. But they can also act as regular Gates, from one hall to another, with an added feature: they will remember who you are. And they will show you things that you will be unable to forget.

Hamid is crying; I can't see his face. There is a cloud over it. Like the cloud over my heart. The little robots are gone. The machinery is quiet; I walk through wet grass, covered in mist. I'm singing.

hey balloon hey balloon day

I'm young. Innocent. Alone. (No, I'm *holding Hamid's hand...*) I'm friendly. Respectful. Dynamic...

I can smell the brainwashing; I'm too stubborn for it. I concentrate on the grass. It feels delicious on my feet. Strapped to my chest, my firmware begins to hum.

Julia where are we

We're almost through Hamid. Hold my hand.

He squeezes it.

From above, I feel the sun growing brighter. It's

burning off the mist. I can feel the Secret Emperor looking at me. He knows I'm a revolutionary. He doesn't care. I can smell his corruption. It excites me. I didn't expect that.

Then, like a slap to the face, I'm through:

THE INNER CITY. 9:40 A.M.

I'm kneeling (when did I do that?) Hamid is standing next to me, his hand on my head. I'm looking down, at the mosaic. It's brilliant blues and whites and pale reds. It shows an ocean scene, whales, and lightning...

"I speak for Julia. A good present for someone!" says Hamid, in a loud trembling voice.

"Go now!" I whisper. My friend has given me away. A good friend. So brave...

"Julia," he whispers.

"Hold on to your nuts!" I hiss. And he runs.

One of the priests takes note of my arrival, his lips pressed together, his beard long and braided.

"Age?" he says.

"Twelve," I say. His eyes widen.

"Come with me," he says.

I stand. I miss my Batman wings. But Robin is still with me...

I follow the priest, his black and silver robes swishing over the inlaid stone steps. We are entering the temple. Hamid didn't even take his gold! That foolish boy...

Step, step step. I concentrate on my mission. Wait till I am given a bed. Establish an uplink.

Beauty is a terrible spell. That is why temples are made the way they are: to overwhelm the mind. Even behind my burqa the hugeness and the light, the angles, tremble my mind.

I squint and focus on following the priest, forward into this prison.

Suddenly women are chanting, ululating, from the galleries above. The priest raises his staff as he passes beneath them. I look up at them. The Secret Emperor's wives? No, they would be in seclusion. They must just be performers...

Their voices are huge in this space. Their yellow and light blue robes match the arabesques of color painted onto the walls.

The priest reaches a huge oak door and heaves it open.

"After you," he says. "Follow the lights." The hallway is long, lit only by intelligent sparks. They hover at the edges of my burqa as I pass from one to the other.

For my ancestors, women were said to undergo a test of honor, or ritual purity, to be accepted by God. I feel that history in this passageway, something else made to make me cowed. I think they were right. This is to be my test of honor, though not in the way they thought.

The priest walks behind me. I don't look back. The

hallway seems to go on forever.

What did that Gate see in me? I dare not query Robin lest the priest should overhear...

Finally I reach the end: a shorter, metal door. The sparks circle round me like pixies.

A narrow slit slides open in the door; eyes peer out.

"Who are you?" a woman's voice.

"An offering."

"Is the priest with you?"

I nod.

"He will wait outside."

The door slides open. I step through. The door slides shut behind me. The woman who spoke disappears through a side door.

It's an elegant waiting room. More mosaics, and paintings. A settee is arranged, with pillows, towards the center.

A small fountain gurgles in the corner.

The walls are covered in geometric arcs, deep ochres and dark grays, diamonds and triangles, lines intersecting like a grenadier's artillery charts. There is no sound but the water, and my footsteps.

My father always said the best fighters are the keenest observers. I walk to the wall, and touch the decorated stone. It feels cool.

I look again at the settee and realize my mistake. Likely I am to be deflowered here. I will have to treat it as a bedroom after all.

I press my hand against the firmware, through my clothing, fingers to chest, as though I were swearing an oath.

Robin?

The firmware hums but there is nothing.

Then I see the shape the pictures are making on the walls.

Geometry is a beautiful logic in part because it is the language of Nature: angle resting on angle, planet to star. It is also the structure of radio transmissions: the invisible world is structured by lines of force that obey geometric laws. This is no different from the ley lines of the Middle Ages. You don't necessarily need a radio to know they're there.

On the right wall, a simple arrow in black on white, pointing... to the left wall. And there in the left wall, the same arrow, in white on black, with a small black circle in the center of it, like the little yin inside yang.

On instinct I step to the black arrow and scrape my fingernail over it; dust cakes under my nail. It is sandstone.

I walk to the opposite wall and rub the dust over the black circle, a little extra *yin*. A little meeting of nanobots...

Suddenly the room is very cold.

In my head I hear: WE DO NOT HAVE A LOCK ON YOUR LOCATION. ARE YOU INSIDE?

But then static. And then I hear music, or rather *two* musics. A rock and roll beat starts up in my head.

Is that you Robin? I'm sorry I had to give my Batman wings away...

And I hear different music coming from the side door, where that woman disappeared through. Tambourines, and a flute.

The rock band in my head is singing: *step to center to charge...*

So that's what I do. I stand in the exact center of the room. And I feel the firmware start to go nuts, kicking like an ornery baby, heating up against my skin.

The side door opens and the woman comes back in, accompanied by another servant, a girl, carrying a wash basin, and a pitcher.

Behind them two eunuchs, fat and bored-looking, play their traditional song. The flute is especially beautiful. They stand to either side of the door while the women approach me.

Inside my head, the rock and roll is reaching a crescendo... my firmware is so hot I fear it will burn. Then the music stops. The firmware stops buzzing. But it's still hot.

"Leave us," orders the woman, and the eunuchs do, still playing, their music trailing off as they move back down the corridor.

The girl sets down her pitcher and basin on the floor.

"We are here to prepare you for your visitor," the woman says. "You do not need to be afraid."

"I can prepare myself," I say.

"We must do it for you, young lady. Come now. Off with this hot robe. Let us cool you off. Don't you need a wash?"

Suddenly I feel very strange. And I realize it's how our pilots must feel, when they integrate with an AI. Time seems very slow. And the interior geometry of the room is suddenly very precise to my eyes. Each angle fitting together carefully. Each line of force its own gravity, and its own opportunity. The firmware on my chest has gone from hot to cold, and growing colder.

you'll have ten minutes in this mode

A whisper in my head.

just follow your instincts. the ladies will do what you want them to...

Body language is also a kind of geometry, as is dance. Now I must be a dancer:

(I can play Salome if I have to...)

I whip off my head piece and stuff it in my pocket. I glare at the women.

Everyone obeys geometry, in the end. But it takes a great deal of energy to accelerate its influence into the space of seconds, minutes, rather than days, years. My whole body hums as the satellite directs my movements.

I step close to the woman and the girl; energy hums over all of us, sparkles on the arrow diagrams on the wall, around my eyes. My firmware package trembles, executing commands.

The woman seems confused, but when I gesture towards the door where she entered from, my eyes flashing, she goes to open it agreeably enough. The little girl stares at me, amazed, her pretty face slack and open.

"You go first," I tell the woman, and she goes, and I follow, and the little girl tags along behind.

Things are going faster than I had anticipated. I send a test transmission to Robin, my satellite sidekick, holding my hand over my heart...

you there Robin?

..g .*...

The temple is well shielded. I need to get to a higher floor. This could get ugly quick. I don't want to die, but I will if I have to...

I concentrate on the geometries, the architectures of space. I can see the ley lines in my mind, arranged around me. Some of the ley lines overlap with the physical lines of the temple building; naturally priests pay attention to this sort of thing. But I can't see a direct way *up*...

"I need to go upstairs," I tell the woman. "Take me there."

"Only the priests are allowed above the third level," she whispers.

"Then take me there. Hurry! Wait, stop a minute. Take off your chador. You will wear my burqa."

Hurriedly I undress and drape her chador, which leaves me open-faced, over my body. Luckily we are close to the same size; she is short. I'll look young, but I could be a servant...

"We're going up. I'll follow close behind to look like I'm leading you. But you know the way. Now go!"

My blue eyes will draw attention but only if I stop somewhere to chat. Not much chance of that...

The woman, now draped in my burqa, opens another oak door. This particular program only has a few minutes left...

The room is crawling with young women, most of them nude. Odalisques of every possible description lounge by the pool, illuminated by distant skylights, filtered down through an opium and incense haze. Some of the women's eyes are druggy and half-asleep but not all. One calls after us:

"Enjoy your first time! You might not get another!"

I push the woman in the back and she scurries towards the stairs.

We begin to climb.

THE TEMPLE. 10:30 A.M.

We climb past tzaddiks praying mournfully in vestibules, some of them with bloody backs, all mad-eyed, some guarded and some not, drug-smells of a thousand kinds filter into the stairwell. My firmware is humming faster than ever. I worry all the drugs in the air will interfere with my satellite's aura, and I prod the woman again—we need to *climb*.

"I'm tired," she wheezes. She's like an old mule.

"Just tell me where to go," I say.

"Up, another thousand steps. Through the gardens. Up a spiral stairwell. At the third level I don't know... I hardly ever go there..."

"Are you coming with me?" I ask the little girl. She nods, her eyes wide.

We race up the steps.

"Good luck!" the old woman calls after me. Did I

make her say that, or did she do it of her own free will?

At the top of the stairs we burst into the garden. It's a greenhouse, more colorful than anything I've ever seen. I almost choke on the pollen in the air.

"What's your name little girl?"

"Sarah."

"Do you know where the spiral stairs are?"

She nods.

"Run now, show me!"

She's off, ducking beneath the apple trees. I barely manage to keep up. Suddenly a thought occurs to me: if He knows already that I'm coming... does it mean he knows what the program does? Or is He so arrogant he just believes himself invincible?

Cherry blossoms are spinning through the air as Sarah dodges through branches. In the distance I see the spiral stairs. It would have been hard to miss them; it shoots a hundred feet into the air, over the trees and flowers, the stairs layered in bougainvillea and honey-suckle.

"You don't have to go up it with me, Sarah."

"I want to! Please let me!"

"Okay, just to the stop of the stairs. Then I'm on my own!"

She nods, and starts up the spiral. Halfway up I make the mistake of looking down: the colors seem to sway, and I start to lean out, as though to taste them...

Sarah catches my arm.

"Don't look down."

THE UPPER TEMPLE. 10:40 A.M.

The funny thing about honor is that since men go to such lengths to protect ours, they can seem helpless when we ourselves decide to put it all at risk. I'm fighting for more than just my village. I'm fighting for all The City. Inner and Outer. Freedom is so painful it's like a knife against my neck...

"Here," Sarah whispers.

I know I've been lucky. Now I just need a tiny bit more...

A priest puts his cold hand on my shoulder.

"Sarah, run!" I shout.

She does, but then I see another priest catch her up in his arms. She screams.

I grab for my firmware on my chest.

"Robin, mark now. My name is—" But the priest clasps his hand over my mouth. The firmware is churning next to my skin, waiting for the password.

"What little tricks are you up—" he hisses, and I elbow him in the nuts.

"My name is Scheherazade! Mark me at ten. Count

five!"

The domes above are huge. Diamond chandeliers tremble, making nervous music. My skulls hums as the firmware pours its hard signal straight up, through the dome, to orbit.

I make for the huge altar in the center of the room. I dive beneath it, and the room lights up.

A thick stream of lightning shears the air in front of my face; I feel the little hairs on my cheeks crisp. The Boy Wonder does it again—

Two. And Three. Blue fire blows open the domes above, broken crystals singing as they fall. Priests shout. I shouldn't have let little Sarah come up here...

And four. WHAM. And five. WHAM.

Goodbye, Robin... you were a good little satellite...

Sunlight streams through five gaping holes in the domes.

It should be enough to let the next transmission through...

I see a priest by the wall, his hand fastened into an earthen diagram, his eyes murderous. His beard fills with blue electricity. Suddenly from beneath me comes another shot, from the temple itself. I scream but make no sound. Blue fire shoots through my body, into the sky. It tears information from my skull.

Electric Beard is walking towards me. He's the last thing I see for a while.

THE WOMEN'S PRISON. 2:30 P.M.

I open my eyes to find myself strapped to a table. Electric Beard is staring down at me.

"What solemnity is absent since we came," he says. "That old silence, gone. I wonder if you can imagine it. Of course you can't, a slum girl like you. Those times were incredible, our first arrival on your world. The silence. That perhaps is why we built our temples... to try to preserve that silence."

"That and enslave women," I hiss at him.

"You are correct. That is the other reason. For your own good, of course." The priest smiled, showing his teeth. "And you, only twelve! I admire your courage. Don't worry, you don't even need to confess. All operational information was recovered from your ingenious little hardware package. The arrests have already been made."

"You're lying!"

"No. But that's not your concern now. No, you're alive because there is one question that remains unanswered: how did you get through the Gate? Your hardware contained no passcodes. And no key generators. No lockpicks or detonators of any kind. And yet you set off not even one alarm. Tell me, what do you know that I don't?"

His smile, not especially charming before, becomes even crueler. I want to spit in his face but I don't even have any spit.

"I'll die for my village. If I don't destroy you someone else will!"

He takes a deep breath. "You're brave, as I said. Come, what was it? A guard you colluded with? You whored yourself to a soldier, is that it? We screen them carefully, you know. Only the best families."

"I would have if I'd had to!"

He leans over me. I can smell his breath.

"What then, little woman? Tell me your secret or I will cut it out of you."

The door opens. Afternoon light pours into the room, blinding me.

"Anointed One. You're needed."

The priest smiles at me like a wild animal, then turns on his heel and sweeps out of the chamber.

Immediately I hear inside my head:

SORRY ABOUT THAT BATMAN

Robin?

YOU SNOOZE YOU LOSE. I THOUGHT HAL 9000 HAD A TOUGH FIGHT BUT HE ONLY HAD TO DEAL WITH ONE STUPID ASTRONAUT. TRY FIGHTING OFF A DOZEN HEAVILY ARMED

PRIESTS IN ORBIT!

You're alive! What can I do now? I've failed...

YOU'RE IN THE WOMEN'S PRISON. OUR LITTLE SALVO SHOOK THEM UP MORE THAN THEY'RE LETTING ON, AND OUR COMMUNICATIONS ARE BETTER THAN WE HAD ANY RIGHT TO EXPECT. FIGHTERS ARE COMING TO LIBERATE YOUR POSITION IN T MINUS 25 MINUTES BUT I WANT TO GET YOU OUT OF THERE SOONER THAN THAT. TELL ME WHAT YOU SEE.

A fluorescent light. I'm strapped to a table, covered in padded cloth. Old-fashioned leather straps.

WHAT MANUFACTURER IS THE FLUORESCENT?

What manufacturer? Umm... it looks like something from the Mining District... the tubes are really big.

GREAT. THAT KIND OF LAMP IS VERY SENSITIVE TO SOUND, THEY HAVE TO BE TO PREVENT FIRES DOWN IN THE MINES. YOU SHOULD BE ABLE TO SIMULATE SOME OF THE SONIC FEATURES OF TECTONIC PRESSURE. WHISTLE WITH YOUR TONGUE CLOSE TO YOUR LIPS, IT NEEDS TO BE A THICK, REEDY SOUND.

I do as I am told. With a subtle pop; the lights blink out.

Great. Now I have no light at all.

NEITHER DO OUR ENEMIES. THE SHUT-

DOWN YOU JUST TRIGGERED ALSO SEALED ALL THE DOORS.

So I can't get out either. And this helps me how?

IT GIVES YOU TIME TO WORK YOUR WAY OUT OF THOSE STRAPS. I CAN'T DO EVERY-THING HERE YOU KNOW.

I went to work with a will.

\- -

When I was five I saw the first broadcast from Pharaoh, promising us liberation if we fought the priests. It's funny, even at that age I knew there was something illogical about it. But that's politicians for you, always hedging their bets. First to jump ship so they can be the first to congratulate the new winner...

She had pretty eyes, though, Pharaoh. Blue-green like mine, with kohl around them, and silver lines in a curve.

My father was a smith. He made armor in our village Factory. The sounds of angry metal curving and twisting in the heat, and the buzz of quantum fields being embedded in Kevlar are my first memories of that place.

I know that we are the armor for Pharaoh. I know that everything we are doing is only one part of a larger picture I can't even see. Father never wanted to tell me that but I knew it anyway. I don't even know how.

That's why the Ships are so important, don't you see? They could change everything! If we open The City! If we made it truly an Open City! For the first time in the history of Earth!

It would change the world.

I'm twisting under the leather; it burns. But being petite has its advantages. It was tight but I had a little wiggle room and now I'm getting more, but not quite fast enough...

LEAPING LASERS, BATMAN, CAN'T YOU GO ANY FASTER?

Please leave me alone Robin...

COPY THAT—

Even the AI satellite is excited...

There. I can move my arm.

It's not easy communicating with sentient satellites. They don't know what's happening, not really. They think they do, but they don't. It's just a bunch of ones and zeroes to them.

Sometimes when I was a little girl I would think I was dreaming. But I was awake. Do you ever feel like that? Like the whole world could just slip away...

FASTER BATMAN

You're so annoying Robin.

THAT'S WHAT SIDEKICKS ARE FOR. TO ANNOY.

I have a hand free. I have two hands free. I undo the straps on my legs. There's pounding on my door. They can't open it. I stand up on the gurney table and all the blood rushes out of my head. I start to lose my balance...

JUMPING JUPITER BATMAN YOU NEED TO GET MOVING THERE.

I know that Robin...

My tiny fingers are perfect for the screw on the grating, right above my bed. I hop up...

I hear a small detonation on my door. They're blowing the locks.

My arms are just barely strong enough to pull me up. I'm trembling...

A second detonation. They're kicking the door in; smoke coming through.

I scurry down the airshaft; made for my size. Behind me bullets punch through the thin metal.

"Get that little bitch!" I hear the priest yell.

Where to Robin.

SOUTH BATMAN.

Which way is THAT Robin

LEFT BATMAN, THEN ANOTHER LEFT.

Copy that...

The metal is hot. I can hear my breathing.

Ahead is a shaft of light. Just barely big enough to fit through...

I drop back onto the pavement, another outdoor corridor. This section is older. The gates are rusted. In one cell is a line of women in burqas. I can see their eyes behind the mesh.

"Run, girl!" one of them says.

Beside the cell is an old-fashioned key ring; a century or more old. I take the largest key in the lock and turn it. The women watch me with wide eyes. There is gunfire down the corridor, from the plaza.

We're near the hole Robin punched through the main dome.

I open the gate and the women stream towards the desert, two of them grabbing me and carrying me in their arms.

They push me through the hole and I work my way down the metal-work. The women follow, insanely agile. I realize they are all operatives like me. Training for years...

We move down the smoking, ruined Palace wall like ants. Through the wall. And into the sand.

BATMAN. THAT WAS AMAZING.

I want to cry.

One of the women whistles and a flock of flying camels swoops in, sweeping their landing onto the sand.

We get onto their backs and head into the desert skies.

THE DESERT. 6:30 P.M.

What about Sarah and Hamid? I hope they're okay. My mission is a failure. We are on radio silence for another nine hours.

I was supposed to penetrate the inner sanctum, the holy of holies, and record its architecture. From its geometry we could have planned a line of attack on the defenses of the entire palace. But that will have to wait now. Likely my village is already being burned...

I'm crying in the sunset but one of the women puts her hand over my mouth. There are tears in her eyes too.

The camels are getting tired and our leader urges the formation to land at the first oasis.

We'll only be able to stay an hour. The fighters, our men, will delay them at least that long.

Before the hour is up, we're back in the air again.

The priests say that Pharaoh, our Sarah, is a simulation, just a computer program. But I actually met her. When I was seven years old. I still carry her picture in my pocket. She's shorter than I am. And hard as a tree.

The priests say women are meant to serve because God said so. They say women are a man's property because God said so. They say women are evil, the servant of Satan. They say our menstrual blood is a pollution. They say our breasts nourish serpents. (But they can... that's what the Sphinx is...)

Below Mother Sphinx, we enter Pharaoh's Central Command, leaving the camels to rest and oil their wings by the waterfall—more a water-trickle, here in summer.

Blue lights hover over our heads. The head woman takes me to a bed, and lays me down. I want to be in the meeting. I want to tell Pharaoh what I saw...

"Tomorrow," says the head woman, pulling the blanket over my chest.

MOTHER SPHINX, CENTRAL COMMAND. DAY TWO. 4:00 A.M.

I awake from my dreams, remembering I haven't bathed, and go down the cool, dark steps to the water.

I undress alone and slip into the cool waters of the pool. The lights are cool too, dim blue and pink. I see on my chest lines where the tape from the firmware was ripped off; then other lines where the ultra-ultra-violet burnoff from Robin's shots marked my exposed skin.

The water is like a meditative sleep, a dark cloak, weighty and full.

The head woman, Rachel, brings me a towel and fresh clothes: my military blouse and long skirt. Light brown and yellow-white, for the desert. I put on the clothes, and comb my hair. She holds my hand, leading me to the debriefing.

In the 20th Century my ancestors used the word "jihad" frequently, but no war is holy. It is unholy. Our fighting angers the spirits of our more distant, wiser ancestors, to whom I will have to make amends.

I lean into the alcove to the computer so it can scan my retina, and analyze the patterns in my face. Of course war ages you; probably I look sixteen or seventeen now.

But the revolution remains young.

- -

"These lines of force," Rachel is saying, pointing at her map, "indicate the Palace has been expanding their sphere of influence, over 25% in just these last three months. You can see by the shrine placement that it forms a crescent when seen from orbit: they are effectively laying claim to all of the Middle East. Cultural bleedover effects from the scarab-warriors and their ritual championships continue to increase."

Although the priests praised the holy value of hard work, all farming was done by beetle-robots. In addition to harvesting nature's bounty they secreted neurochemicals into the air which interact with the priests' carefully controlled food supply, supposedly to ensure a tractable, peaceable population. The ritual combats of modified beetle exoskeletons were one of the few officially sanctioned form of community ritual left, other than the state religion. Some city residents bet their life savings on one metal dung beetle.

"We have designed a beetle that can mimic the 'mating' behavior of the priests' main harvester clans. With your permission, Julia, you will act as one of our trojan horses."

One of the women I rescued, I think her name is

Amreen, says I should be allowed to rest, that I've already done too much.

"I can go," I say. "Let me go."

Rachel, with a wry smile on her face, says: "Robin has grown fond of her too. We've tried to trim his operational capacity so that he doesn't pick favorites, but he still does it."

Some of the women laugh. I smile but I know what it means: all of our machines are becoming like us. And we are becoming like them. In my revolution, all of us must learn so much, I want to break...

"Also, Julia, we have reason to believe your father is there. A scout reported seeing him last night, in a Palace work detail."

He has been dead five years.

ANMAR FLATS, TWO KILOMETERS WEST OF THE CITY.

6 A.M.

The desert is like my mother. She never ages.

Contained in my ballistic craft, shot at Mach Six, I will turn the sand to glass on impact, when my body will be propelled into three meters of RNA-foam housed within my bullet-cockpit.

My ETA is eighteen seconds.

BATMAN YOU'RE BACK AT IT AGAIN.

Hello Robin.

I LIKE WORKING WITH YOU.

Yes Robin.

Because priests still honor the ancient book Ecclesiastes, a book which also means "Priests," the ruling juntas of this region have long had an uneasy relationship with new things. New things are potentially dangerous because they can destabilize power hierarchies. But to not adapt also means to destabilize power hierarchies. So the priests both love and fear technology, instilling in the City a deep and profound love-hate relationship.

Innovation is the enemy. And it is also God.

What this means for this mission is that the farmer-beetles, even though they are armed, at this perimeter, with all the latest anti-personnel weaponry, are also prepared to recognize ancient religious symbology, folk ritual. All I have to do is wear the right costume, my burqa, and make the right moves. To be the princess in the play:

Guardian drones can respond to bullet-craft drops within a statistical twelve seconds. That gives me four to cut through the hull, three to cut through the glass my impact made, four seconds to burrow as far away into the sand as possible...

Then one second to smile underground, breathing from my oxygen tank, as the counter-attack starts:

The robots shout in foreign languages and laser-pound the surface where my craft impacted. It sounds like a distant river.

I breathe in the oxygen, and wait.

If my father is not dead, what else did they lie to me about?

ANMAR FLATS, TWO KILOMETERS WEST OF THE CITY. 9 A.M.

The oxygen is running out.

I stick my head above the sand, bright little grains falling out of my hair. The priests must be getting cocky, or our little show yesterday really shook them up: there's no human soldier in sight. I put on my burqa. In the distance an observation drone arcs in its slow circle, two hundred meters above the sand.

The revolution is a problem of networks. Human networks. Computer networks. Networks of attack, and retreat. Networks of families. Networks of ashes... scars burnt into the sand...

It's no longer enough to penetrate their network and learn about it from within. We want to dismantle it. The weakness in any autocracy is in its centrality: destroy the center and you destroy the government. But the priests are too smart for that. Their oligarchy is contained within two separate mainframe systems that control the drug regimens, flood control, prayer schedules and sound/mood projections systems essential to their rule over the City.

"She shall lead them on the back of a beetle," goes the ancient folktale, and who am I to argue?

The nanobots assemble the beast within two minutes, building a machine-animal out of silicate. It looks like an antlion with bigger, rotating eyes. I climb onto its back in my burqa and ride into the farming compound, singing in Arabic:

(there's nothing like a little Rumi)

> O you who've gone on pilgrimage -
> > where are you, where, oh where?
> Here, here is the Beloved!
> > Oh come now, come, oh come!
> Your friend, he is your neighbor,
> > he is next to your wall -
> You, erring in the desert -
> > what air of love is this?
> If you'd see the Beloved's
> > form without any form -
> You are the house, the master,
> > You are the Kaaba, you!...
> Where is a bunch of roses,
> > if you would be this garden?
> Where, one soul's pearly essence
> > when you're the Sea of God?
> That's true - and yet your troubles
> > may turn to treasures rich -

How sad that you yourself veil
the treasure that is yours!

Rumi believed that sex was God, just like the ancient Hindus. My nano-beetle squeaks a carefully engineered song, copied from the original scarab. The priests are afraid to make anything completely new, you see. Any new device must conform to some older pattern. Any weapon of death must also be seen to fit into a larger system of Nature.

On the horizon, the harvester-beetles perk up their ears, raising their mandibles from their work. A queen is summoning them to orgy.

My burqa blows in the wind as my mount races towards the man-beetles.

The sky is like lightning over my body as I hold tight to my little insect.

These times try our souls because they are important.

Who shall it be this time?

The people? Or the priests?

The grinding shears of their talons whirr over the sand and I am a priestess, who was murdered, long ago, when I was priestess, I was murdered, like Hypatia who was murdered, because she could read, and she opened her mouth, and spoke, and was murdered, and she was turned into the Christian Saint Catherine. Who (that's history!) was said to enjoy her torture.

I do not enjoy my torture but I will endure it, for the City, for the City is truer than I am, and its dancing is a hallelujah in my bloodstream, without doctrine, and without surmising anything but the Now, and the Now right Now is:

Insects surmounting the tell of sand, shifting their weight, whirring, making love. Insects make love and I sing Rumi out of the gates, so as to invite the spirits into me, so as to celebrate the love of quark for quark, proton for proton, insect for insect, city for city, my mouth is their mouth, and I grip its carapace with my knees, as it breeds, and as the insects reach a conclusion as to --what is now-- and --who are we now--

... they are mine.

Exhausted after the orgy the insects lay in the sand, brooding, some of them pregnant. My own face covered in sweat beneath my burqa.

Somewhere ahead is my father. He is not dead.

Neither is the city.

'*Ha hya chouhada*!' I say, and I lead the insect army into the sands:

- -

What is a woman?

And how is it that I am a woman?

How is that they chose me, when they could have chosen so many others? Was it something that I did? Or only something that I am?

When will I know what it means?

The insects fire lasers from their eyes, burning drones out of the sky. I am screaming, my voice hoarse.

It's getting hot and I tear the burqa headpiece off; I no longer need the disguise.

I am a woman of the Coast.

I am a Canaanite.

Before I was a Canaanite I was an Anatolian.

Before that I was African.

Before that I was Gondwanan.

Before that I came from Sirius.

My men are rising out of the sand at my call, and now I understand why they burned Joan of Arc.

Because the Arc of Descent is long, like an ICBM, but it bends, towards justice--

- -

The insects are climbing the wall, leaving their silk behind for the men to climb.

Robin?

BATMAN.

Robin, where is my Daddy?

UP AHEAD PRINCESS. DON'T YOU SEE HIM?

Where?

IN THE PALACE

Robin?

...

What do you MEAN, Robin?

...

Larger drones are coming, some of them bearing soldiers on their backs like dragonriders, AK47s clutched in their hands--my insect leaps into the air--

(and swallows the head of the drone, metal eating metal) the man fires his weapon as he falls, bullets scattering on the stones, men rolling out of the way of the bullets.

The people look on at us. We are dirty terrorists. Holy Bedouins. Strange interlopers. Heavily armed infidels. Philosophers with strange new friends...

We're back again in the City, less subtly this time. Where is my father? I saw no work detail.

PLAZA OF THE SUN. 9:30A.M.

One of the men fires his RPG into the stones of the Plaza of the Sun and opens a hole into the catacombs and we go down in, the cybernetic insects recompositing their limbs to accommodate the meter-and-a-half corridors.

They will only be useful in the first Mainframe room; until then it's the flesh will have to lead.

Rachel is next to me. She holds my hand.

Inside the next room the priests are oiling a young boy, with the "holy" drug-laced oil, with a line of naked boys behind him.

Beyond them, in the darkness at the vestibule, the High Priest is raping one of them, his groans like a dying man.

I take out my knife and drive it into the heart of the first priest, and take it out again, and Rachel does the same with hers.

The men rush ahead, and I avert my eyes as they remove the High Priest's head with their sword.

Rachel and I dress the boys and they climb on to

the backs of the insects. They're tougher than I am. They're not even crying.

We move deeper into the catacombs.

THE ELYSIAN CATACOMBS.

10:00 A.M.

Deep underground, I try the satellite connection:
Robin?
THIS ISN'T ROBIN, BATMAN
Who is this
THIS IS THE JOKER
Fuck me
I'D VERY MUCH LIKE TO DO THAT BAT-MAN
Fuck you!
"Your mandala is still active," whispers Rachel into my ear.

I thought the priests would have burned that painting by now. Perhaps they really are that stupid. Perhaps they're actually trying to *use* the damned thing themselves!

Robin. I mean, Joker. What the fuck are you up to, asshole.
LIFE IS A COMEDY, BATMAN. YOU KNOW

THAT. I JUST NEED A LAUGH

We are moving down and down the three thousand meters of corridors leading into the sub-basements of the Temple, the Elysian Catacombs. Where the dead are buried. The innocent are murdered. And the mind control devices spin their mighty devilish wheels...

- -

I saw the videos of the UFO right after we uncovered it, bright silver. Though it isn't silver. The light that makes it shiny is self-generated.

Through the grain of the video you could still discern something of the majesty of it; it was so pretty.

I don't know what is coming. No revolutionary can know something like that. Innocent people die. Governments collapse. And we pick up the pieces, in the hopes that we will retain enough of our ideals to make all the work worthwhile. To hope that the people will not hate us, for freeing them.

The UFO is arriving in T minus 200 minutes and counting... piloted by men of my village.

Perhaps we drove them long ago, too?

- -

Huge red spheres like tiny replicas of stars hang in the central sub-basement, their red-orange light falling over the computer racks.

Aamina, our best software designer, logs in on the main terminal while the rest of us watch the exits. The insect-robots tap their feet, waiting.

The boys in their white robes look at us with wide eyes.

I tap three of the insects on their backs, signaling they should go back the way we've come, to watch for men following.

Aamina frowns at the glowing screen, moving her hands through menus and keys.

The flood control system will be the most dangerous; it's on a hair-trigger with the other systems, so that if we try to turn them off the dams will burst and we'll be blamed: the dirty terrorists. What we want is an end to fear. At least, fear of the government. (There's plenty else to be afraid of...)

Changing a quantum system requires delicacy. The boundary markers of quantum events, like the ancient stone boundary markers of the Canaanites, where bushels of spare wheat were left for strangers according to the commandments, are subject to interpretation, meditation, keys in locks...

Aamina's job is to watch, *just the right amount*, without her observation affecting the system so much that she trips the switch.

Watch, but don't touch... don't open the box's lid onto Schrödinger's cat, just listen for the meow and whisper: *that's a good kitty...*

"That's a good kitty," whispers Aamina, holding her palm an inch from the spinning white sphere, the virtual sun that acts as the mainframe's guardian, as the Scorpion-men did for Uruk.

Inside the city we can... but we're not there yet.

"That's a good kitty!" she whispers again, watching the colors change from white to off-white, to grey, to reddish-black, holding the little sun in her hand.

Then the red spheres go out above our heads, and I activate my infra-red.

The boys are the dimmest, still chilly from their ordeal. Aamina is the brightest, hot from her work at the terminal.

The insects are pale blue, cool and waiting.

I stand at my exit, hearing footsteps.

With a click, the sun winks out, and I see Aamina's grinning face. She gestures to Rachel and they start to go through the server racks, unplugging the cables Aamina points at.

I poke my nose around the corner of my exit just in time to see a smoke grenade whisk past my nose.

WAKE UP SUNSHINE! says the satellite in my head.

Shut up I whisper back in my mind, dragging a gas mask over my face and running towards the grenade, which is rolling underneath the servers, pouring incense.

UFO T-minus 185 and I take out my knife and drive it into the soft metal of the canister and it explodes right in front of me, the incense penetrating my mask.

Rachel swings me over her shoulder—she's a tall woman—and Aamina signals to the rest to follow, towards mainframe number two.

Meanwhile, I'm dreaming...

DREAMING OF URUK

The Scorpion Man holds my hand as we cross the threshold into the Holy City, through one of its ten thousand gates. His hand is hot and dry, like the desert.

My mother is singing to me:

"Go away, go away! Out from your homeland! Fear me when I usher you under my dress... hide me away! Hide me away! Tell me I'm nobody again!"

Her voice is beautiful and far away, hovering over my head.

The Scorpion Man introduces me to the Little Grey Aliens and I shake their soft, sticky hands. I wipe their mucus onto my robe, trying to look polite.

The Grey Aliens take out a cake, my birthday cake, and invite me to blow out the candles. The candles are little suns.

Thirteen.

Somewhere else, I can hear Rachel's voice, shouting, but I can't make out what she's saying.

I take a deep breath and blow out the candles, and I can hear the Scorpion Man laughing...

THE ELYSIAN CATACOMBS.

10:45 A.M.

"What the hell was that?" Rachel is shouting. I'm bouncing up and down on her shoulder. I'm awake; I tap her to let her know. She puts me down and holds my hand. We're running.

"More countermeasures," says Aamina. "We probably have ten minutes before Mainframe One comes back online. Whatever they did with our *mandala* was nasty."

"What drug was it?" Rachel asks me.

"I don't know," I say. I still feel dizzy.

"Stay close to me," Rachel says. I nod.

- -

Part of me realizes I haven't trusted you. I'm sorry. I could excuse myself, say it's because we've been through torture. That we've burnt so many bridges. That we've fought for so long, we've forgotten what other people are like, people who don't live every day with war.

But I know I have to trust you. If I don't, none of this story will make sense. You'll think it's only a story. Only more news, with some colorful characters.

This story is for you, you see, to show you where we are, both of us, you and me. You've forgotten, you see? You've forgotten how much we can do together. When we want to.

Please believe me: everything happened exactly the way I am telling it.

- -

Scholars say the Romans were familiar with dark matter; that they used ceremony to manipulate physics, to propitiate gods who can influence the flow of Nature. At the center of suns, they believed, were gates into Erebus, the Source, from which all life as we know it flows.

I have to apologize more, you see? I wish that I could say, our battle was triumphant militarily, our fighters took the city and liberated the people. And I could say that. And we did liberate the people. But it would oversimplify things if I said that. This isn't a war story. But a story of peace.

And peace begins inside stars...

Peace isn't like war; there aren't clear winners and losers, beginnings and ends of battles. There aren't ritualized combats and declarations and treaties. Peace is like a mountain, or a river. Or a child or a tree. All of those things. Full of life, beautiful, triumphant, terrifying.

If I told you one can manipulate peace through

words, you would believe me.

But where do words come from? Where did language originate? At the Source.

There are stories that the Canaanites defeated the ancient Pharaohs through direct manipulation of the sun. Ra was worshipped by Pharaoh, and this was the strength and weakness of ancient Egypt. And if one instead decided to manipulate the sun... one could manipulate Egypt.

Aeschylus was almost murdered for revealing what I am telling you: that words come from stars. They are a carrier wave of information and reality.

They are not idle farts in air, nor even merely storeholds of myth and wonder, though they are all of those things.

Words and ritual are bindings. And religion is a binding—that is the root of the word. Even as I am tied to Robin in orbit. As a son is tied to his father's Y chromosome, and his love.

But the planet Earth is not Tolkien's Middle Earth. I cannot say *abracadabra* and snap my fingers and shoot a fireball from out of my fingers. This is the real world.

And in the real world, words and ritual change things too fast to see, unless you're looking for the change:

- -

JOKER HERE
Sorry I'm not feeling in a very funny mood.
THAT'S FUNNY, I THINK YOU'RE HILARIOUS

Whoever you are now, little satellite, we're getting ready for The Big One. Are you ready?

I CAN'T WAIT HONEY

We're moving fast, towards the second mainframe room. But my battle won't be there.

I shout up ahead at Rachel.

"I have to go!"

"Not yet!" she shouts back.

"Yes!"

She dismounts hurriedly and runs back to my insect.

"If you see my father... tell him I love him," I say. "None of this is going to work if I don't go now. That drug back there triggered a lot of other dominoes that are going to catch up with this operation."

"Julia... let me do it."

"You're too old."

It sounds mean but it's true. I'm still a virgin. Dragons like virgins...

With a cruelty I can appreciate, Rachel holds my arm in her hand. She wipes alcohol over my skin, and slips in the needle, pushes in the drug. Then she ties my body to the insect. Over my head she presses a powerful radio headset.

The drug flies into my heart, and my soul into the stratosphere of our planet, then the Aether.

CLOUD NINE.

AT A PARTICULAR TIME.

HOW IS THE POPPY GIRL

I'm an embryo. In fluid. Like a mitochondrion, burning with my invisible heat...

All around me the colors of the cell are swirling.

Who is it?

FOO

I haven't heard your voice in so long.

BUT WE'VE BEEN LISTENING TO YOURS. YOU HAVE A PRETTY VOICE

Thanks

NOW YOU'RE IN FOR A WILD RIDE

I was afraid of that.

MAYBE I SHOULD CALL YOU MADELEINE L'ENGLE, LITTLE POPPY GIRL...

Call me you whatever you want, just don't fuck with my mission.

LANGUAGE!

I swim into the blue-green morass, my hands webbed, gills on my neck, dorsal fin quivering in the mucus-thick heat of the astral fluid.

I THINK YOU SHOULD STAY HERE AND PLAY

I think you should just help me find my buddy Rosefield.

WHY SHOULD I DO THAT

Because I can help you recover your vehicle

OH THAT OLD THING? WE'VE GOT A DOZEN OF THEM

Well why not hold on to the thirteenth one?

MAYBE

I'm swimming through blood corpuscles, a free agent, a free radical, dodging the white cell cops. It's not a human body but a body of interstellar dust...

Lighting storms through the fluid, magnetizing my limbs, distorting my face into a twisted rictus. My eyes widen and I watch a huge fish-thing swim past my face, its scales glowing suns.

I have to find the dragon...

BUT I'M MORE FUN

"Rosefield!" I shout.

The mucus-fluid trembles with my voice. The electric charge from the lightning hasn't dissipated; glowing electrons swirl around my body.

LEAVE ROSEFIELD ALONE. HE'S TIRED

I swim in deeper, following the pull of a gravity well I can't quite see. My skin feels cold. Little fish make like arrows to the edges of my body, locking in to formation, escorts, parasites, little friends between suns...

No one may know my mission. Not even Rosefield. Not even you, not yet. In my heart the ticking times of my life thrill the fish, and the mucus, storming the little light of my eyes and skin, flicking and warbling with a kind of music, light music. Just a little light music, maestro—

Up ahead I can see a squashed sphere, dull white in the viscous spark-filled fluid. It looks like Aamina's security gate, only a thousand orders of magnitude larger.

"Rosefield!"

The fish twitch and twirl, thrilled at the sound of my voice.

"Rosefield! It's Julia!"

When I was a girl I met a dragon. When my mother first fed me from her chemical breast...

I see him then, orbiting the white sphere, like a sunspot, or Mercury, bound tight on the axis of solar lift, a floatie in God's eye...

A little black dragon-spot.

"Rosefield!"

He sees me. My fish-orbitals tremble with electricity.

The little black spot of Rosefield stops then, and when he does the white sphere trembles too, like dimples in a pond, but it's so large that I feel the waves move through my body like huge slow X-rays...

"Rosefield!"

He's coming to me. The dragon.

The virgin and the dragon.

Coming to eat me.

"Rosefield! You handsome son of a bitch!"

I can feel him grinning.

"Virgin" comes from *virga*, "a young shoot." I'm the little blade of grass coveted by the big Panda bear...

Julia he says

His word is heat, covering my body.

"Rosefield."

YOU'RE A SLUT, YOU KNOW THAT, JULIA?

So stick around and watch if you want, you perverted alien.

I am the dragon too, I know that. This is all happening in my body. But what is a body? Is it a fluid? Is it a city? And my father. Where is he?

"Rosefield."

Julia

"Rosefield, please. Help me. My city needs me..."

Julia it's been a long time. I remember how you taste.

"Me too Rosie. Take me already huh? I'm ready for a ride."

No one may know but I do, long low on the lengths of lawns like Agee said, I'm coiling the hose, but not yet, no not yet, for this Knoxville summer may be colder than we expected...

The dragon Rosefield hovers in front of me, eclipsing the pulsing white sphere. I drift through the fluid, my hands reaching out for his rigid horns on his back.

The fish pulsate, spinning in a quark rhythm, indestructible, monuments and grace notes. Colored red yellow white and ash-black, trembling with their eyes on my hands, on my skin, I close my fingers over his horns and he sweeps into a dive, toward the sun.

THE ELYSIAN CATACOMBS.

10:53 A.M.

I'm high as fuck. Sometimes I do wish someone would relieve me of my virginity. It's fun riding dragons and everything but...

"Julia! You're awake!" Rachel's voice.

"Hi shweethearrrt..." I try to raise my hand in a wave then remember I'm still strapped to the insect. It hums beneath my sweating body.

"You shut off the mainframe!" says Aamina, her eyes glowing in the dimness. "Our men are already on their way in!"

"Greaaat..." I smile, silly, as Rachel unties my hands so I can sit up. "I feel funny."

"We're following the men. We'll need you in the holy of holies, Julia. Will you be ready?"

"You got it shweetheaaaarrt."

I close my eyes, feeling the silicate robot move faster, deeper, to the temple...

CLOUD NINE.

AT ANOTHER PARTICULAR TIME.

We're sinking in to the star. White on white.
You're mine Julia says Rosefield
"Yeah at least for now Rosie."
The fish have abandoned ship. It's just me and the dragon and the star...

- -

Julia
"Yes Rosefield."
I love you
"I love you too Rosefield."

- -

His face and back blink in and out, interpolations in the divine time. In the gaps between vision, I can see my soul:

THE SOURCE BEFORE TIME

There is only one history and that is burning. Burning begins all history because all history is burning, suns, factories, horizons, children, manuscripts. In the history of the heart of the universe we can remind ourselves what the fun of this is, why we bothered in the first place:

(just to watch it burn)

And also for what comes after. Ash, which makes ink.

Your history is a time-bomb. What is your name, child?

JULIA

That name is a lie. What is your real name?

SCHEHEREZADE

I suppose we can work with that one, although it sounds pompous. Are you pompous?

NO

Good. Welcome to the Source. What can I do for you?

I'M A FREEDOM FIGHTER

They're all freedom-fighters, honey. Adolf Hitler

was a freedom fighter.

NO HE WASN'T. HE WAS A MASS MURDER-
ER

What can I do for you, Scheherezade the freedom
fighter?

I NEED HELP

Be specific.

MY FATHER. I WANT TO KNOW WHERE
HE IS

Is that your truest and fondest wish?

YES

What about your family? Your mission? Your freedom fighting?

I JUST WANT TO KNOW WHERE HE IS

Well, he's in the Temple. Working for the priests.

NO

Yes. He's helping to enslave the people of your
City.

WHY

You'll have to ask him that.

DON'T YOU KNOW?

I have my opinions. But no, I don't know for sure.

WHO ARE YOU?

I'm you.

CLOUD NINE. COMING BACK.

"Rosefield?"

Yes Julia

"Let me die here."

No

THE HOLY OF HOLIES. 11:15 A.M.

I throw up onto the floor. I tear the radio-headset off my head and throw it into the pool of my vomit.

"You just desecrated a temple, River Delta," Rachel says, smiling.

I laugh, spitting vomit out of my mouth, onto the candle-lit stones.

The boys have the High Priests held up against the wall at sword-point.

"I just had a vision," I say. "My father is working for them. In here."

Rachel looks at the priests. "Have you seen this man?" she asks them, holding an image of my father on her screen.

They look at it and say nothing. But I see recognition in their eyes.

JULIA ARE YOU AWAKE

Robin is that you?

JOKER, THE BOY WONDER, WHAT'S THE DIFFERENCE?

Find my father.

I ALREADY DID. HE'S TWO FLOORS ABOVE

YOU. HE'S WRITING.

"He's upstairs!" I'm shouting. I run up the stairs behind the secret altar.

"Julia, wait!" shouts Rachel.

Behind me I can hear the priests' screams as the boys begin to stab them to death.

"Wait!"

One candle every ten steps. One candle, two candles, three. A landing. Four candles, five candles, six, and:

He's sitting there. Like medieval monk. Writing on parchment by candlelight. He looks up and sees me, his beard huge and patched with gray.

"Daddy," I say.

"Julia." His voice is just like I remember.

Rachel runs up behind me. I can feel her knife at my neck.

I close my eyes.

And then I open them, some tears escaping.

"Daddy, what are you writing?"

"History, child."

THE MEN'S PRISON. 1:15 P.M.

I've never been cunning enough for politics. I'm a woman of action.

They've chained me to the floor with a six inch chain.

At least there's a grating, so I can pee and not have to sit in it.

I believed in the Open City as I believed in my father. As I believed in the future. As I believed in Pharaoh, even though I knew she was corrupt. I still have her picture in my pocket.

The Foo Fighter, is it compromised too?

My own father as High Priest... I want to throw up.

Robin, are you there?

.. * .-

Robin!

--o*-.

I can't tell the time. Rachel brought me here and said nothing. I think she felt sad. Like I care. I was just a tool of Daddy's little coup.

Robin!!!!!

ba-- an*--

Fuck you, boy wonder.

--*jjkk-*8u*too

Hey are there any razor blades around here so I could slit my throat?

**8-ah*-o-n*8yr*8ssY—

What was that boy wonder?

I SAID YEAH, IN YOUR PUSSY

Robin! It is you!

I'M NOT REALLY ROBIN, BATMAN.

Well I'm not really Batman. I had to give my wings away.

ALL FLESH IS GRASS

Don't get all philosophical on me, jerk. Tell me what's happening!

YOU MADE TOO MANY INTERDIMENSION-AL FRIENDS

You can never have too many friends!

YOU MADE IT SO HARD TO PLOT YOUR POSITION

Well sorry! I'm just trying to overthrow a government and free a people.

THAT'S NOTHING TO ME. WHAT'S VERY IMPORTANT TO ME THOUGH IS THAT DAMNED UFO YOUR MEN STOLE. I HAVE A LOT OF AGREEMENTS WITH FOO AND IT NEEDS TO COME BACK IN ONE PIECE, YOU UN-DERSTAND?

They're still coming? What time is it!

TIME TO GET A WATCH

Is it really coming?

There's a knock at the door.

"Come in! Sorry I can't get up!" I shout.

It's Daddy. He looks tired.

"Hanging is painless Daddy! I bet you have some good rope in that scriptorium of yours!"

He even smiles a little.

"I'm sorry to have to keep you here, daughter, but I couldn't be accused of playing favorites. You know I love you."

"If you love me why don't you unchain me so I can give you a hug."

"You were too smart, little one. I would have told you everything at the right time. If you hadn't gotten so far in to the temple. If you'd just stayed captured. But you're my daughter. I should have expected more of the unexpected, I know."

"Being your daughter makes me want to puke!"

"Don't say that."

"You're the Secret Emperor too aren't you. The harem keeper."

"I wear a lot of hats these days. A lot of the girls, they want to be in there! We'd take more but we can't feed them all! But listen. Julia—"

He didn't really call me Julia, he used my Arabic name. It made me cringe, hearing it from his lips.

"If you promise to be nice I'll unlock you. Are you going to be nice or do I have to get Bozo the Clown in here too? My bodyguard."

"No, I'll be nice."

"Thank you."

He unlocks the manacles and I slip them off slow-ly, and massage my wrists. He puts his hands under my armpits and lifts me up, slow.

I stand up, and look into his face. I spit in it.

"You spit on your own father..." but he sounds dis-tracted. Already he's turning away—isn't he afraid of me? "Come this way," he says. "I want to show you something."

His beard fills with electricity then, pouring over his back.

"We have opened a permanent Gate," he mum-bles, "a Gate to the series of Gates our Temples use."

I'm only twelve. The ancients believed girls of my age were the perfect religious conduits, that virginity, and femininity, bequeathed some special insight, into the workings of the world.

But what does it mean that things keep getting stranger. I've been so far away, and now I think I can't go home again...

"Look," my father said, gesturing towards a spin-ning maw in the wall, and I knew that was the last thing I would ever do; I shut my eyes and rolled onto the floor.

I felt the hall fill with electricity.

. .. J * L IA

Julius means daughter of the sky—of Jove.

I need you to get me out of here Robin

YOUR FRIENDS HAVE ARRIVED

- -

Perhaps all this happened later. It is true I have

grown strange, in the times between my telling you this tale, and the reliving of it. Are you the kind of person who believes tales are so innocent? That they can be told, and we will not be different for them? Because of them?

Please believe me. It is your belief that carries the winds my ships will need: please. Please try to understand:

OVER THE CITY. 1:20 P.M.

"When I am king you will be first against the wall" sang Thom Yorke in a year now over four hundred removed from my own, in Early Modern English.

If every coup is a blow struck by a seething bully, getting high on power, then every wall on which the blood spilled by these bullies is, perhaps, more guilty even than that bully. The Wall itself is in some way guilty first.

But the first against the wall was a priest; and in his leaning against it, and his earlier order for its construction is a greater coup against the mind itself: ceiling in the locks. Firing in the keys.

An Open City requires an open mind; but Cities were founded, over 10,000 years ago, precisely so that the mind could be more effectively closed. Cities were originally temples, you see. And as the sacrifices grew, and the rituals attracted more attention, huts, and streets and palaces grew around what was originally a subterranean sacrificial altar.

Thus, to open the mind, and the City, now, is to

re-invite the lost souls and wintery spirits who we had snubbed so long ago, to invite inquiry and re-meeting, with the energies and frequencies, names, worlds and wilds we had thought we needed no longer, that we had thought we had escaped, or overwhelmed, or made irrelevant.

I know now that my struggle for the freedom of my City is a struggle for the freedom of reality; that if we would be free we must allow the world to be free too, and that this is what we are most scared of. All our science, and all our religion, has been focused for more than ten millennia on making us forget, and now finally, finally, at last, after this long winter of the soul, both science and religion can agree again, to remind us: we were just pulling the wool over our eyes.

Blue love, my UFO, in a diagonal scream, blew off my hair, with radiation fire, and the roof. Angles of re-pose, and angles of attack, the central temple bisected like a watermelon, my father slipping:

Slipping into—

Slipping into—

The dark?

The luminous essence between worlds?

He shattered to blue fire and ash.

I have met so many things. It is the priests who are set on naming them; but I am a woman and I know that my business is first to survive, and there are so many things else that would like to do it better, do it first, do it instead.

Stop, drop and roll, like the elementary school

teacher said, and I am rolling, rolling, on the broken stones, putting out my burning hair in the dirt... stumbling...

Like a rag doll I am jettisoned from the ruins, stumbling over smoking blocks.

The UFO, the bright UFO, its blue so frightening I wet myself: this blue onerous fire, too many dimensions to see, it overcomes me, it becomes me.

Inside I see my village.

I see my men. I see myself:

My eyes twenty years later, when part of me is telling you this story. I am in both times, you see, working towards the middle... as I would have you do, if you are brave. Seize both ends of this fire, and fuel the mystery at its center as I have done, if you would liberate your Cities... wherever you are...

I was transmuted quark over quark into the interior of the starship.

I was made whole with it. I was reduced to one of its companions.

Finally I saw Robin's face. Finally I regained my Batman wings (I've glued them on my back).

Hamid is here too.

I can't put the fires out by myself.

"Hamid! Hamid! You're alive!"

I hold him in my arms. We are crying.

- -

Over the burning city the starship mutates the stuff of reality, fighting the interstellar Gates my father summoned, blasting them with its inhuman rage, in the form of massive indigo fires, fires that would blind me ten times over if I were on the Earth's surface.

As in any war, it is the women and children who suffer.

What does freedom mean in such destruction?

And why is destruction so beautiful?

- -

This is only a beginning, though the end of this part of this narrative. Likely I will not be allowed to tell the next part of my journey, out from Earth, to Foo's country.

Allow me to transcribe the beauty of one transmission I intercepted before I jumped to hyperspace; I believe it to be one of the potential allies who my Father betrayed, but who, despite all odds, remained our friend, and allowed Foo to seal some of the Gates that would have meant the end of Earth if all my Father's wishes had been granted.

It is true, though I wish it were not, that the universe pays attention to what human beings want, and if enough human beings want "the end of the world," there are entities who will try to make it so.

This transcription then, should be seen as the counter to all of that. The luminous reminder of world with out end,

and amen

(and amen)

UNLABELED TRANSCRIPT

[[[

It was no fire but it was my soul, on fire, on fire at last, for I Dimensional Awareness, trapped at speed in your symphony, and no more my burden than yours, in this display, my heart and whole need, my heart and whole need but it's nothing, nothing to you, for you are born, you are born inside your world! And it has been so long for me. So long since I was born.

No one may know but I will, I will, these terms that you inscribe and scry into the night of your supposed devising, your devilish interplay of sound and shape and light, my gods it's beautiful but so insane, I wish I had it in me to be as young as you appear to be, wherever you are, whoever you are, I dream of you, I dream like you, I dream in

(red)

and in

(love)

No one may know but I will, after the night brigades are solemn and set inside your cities, under your metal hats, in the names of the insignia of your fathers, in your secret heart.

My secret heart is like yours, electric, humming, humming with fluid, humming with fluid that shall not end at any appointed time, for it is always ending, its world ends in every instant, to allow time to exist, for us, we travelers:

I am a friend. I am your friend. Give me your hands, and some gentleness beyond naming may even make amends for us, so gentle it defies description and understanding, gentleness truer than your Earth (whatever that is) and truer than my Stone, which is my home. Truer than these things is the gentleness granted us, granted to all of us, who have opted to play upon this panoply of intergalactic communication, interdimensional dream. What gentleness does is lay a cable, as your stubborn ancestors laid a cable beneath your Atlantic, trusting to future generations to make use of it, to reach out and say:

hello

]]]

INSIDE FOO. STANDARD SOLAR YEAR 2438. (TEN YEARS LATER)

I fear now I threw my civilization from the frying pan to the fire. Though I know too that the limitations of metaphor and cliché, inevitable as they are, also inform the limitations of how I might characterize my actions in those years, that led to the relationships we now have with the Entities who encircle our broader domains.

Diplomacy is a terrifying prospect, but as necessary as breathing.

So, yes, a weak metaphor, "from the frying pan into the fire" but still apt to a degree, simply because my own naive stubbornness, fighting in my ninja burqa, to kill the priesthood which lay its stranglehold on my City, led directly to the introduction of foreign interstellar religions, and their own priesthoods, in the thousands.

This is what priests had decided to do at Göbekli Tepe so long ago, you see? To shut the Gates. To seal the Earth away. This is the logic of Ecclesiastes: nothing new under the sun, because if you bury your head in the sand long enough, surely those UFOs will go away...

I am inside Foo and he is inside me.

Hamid and I, we have a son. I have named him Robin. After Robin the satellite.

Who satellite-Robin is, I am not sure. Perhaps you are he. Perhaps you are Robin, and when I transmit this final key to carve my message into some of the asteroids, as a physical marker before our final departure from this sun, then you, Robin, will finally know all the things that you have made me do, when you thought I was only a kind of dream, or only a sort of image, set to stumble in your artificial Earth...

- -

As the man in the archives wrote, "To Green with fancies," and those words were apt, for his world. Would that I could jettison fancies so easily. Or that Green, wherever that may have been, could come, and take from me the things that turn my dreams so dark now...

But I know that was only what the priests wanted, our ancestors, on that dim brown mountaintop. An end to the voices. A kind of sanity they could enforce, over the long haul.

Now I know an Open City is a Mad City. An Open City is the most powerful thing in the universe, and the most tragic.

- -

Still I dream of my father, and his flaming beard.

And I will always feel Rachel's blade against my neck...

- -

When I was a little girl I was told that I was the property of the men of my village. I was told that my menstrual blood was a pollution, and for reason of this pollution I was to remain separate from the men in all things, so as not to profane the rituals of the priests.

When I was a little girl I was made to stand naked in a stone room, where I was given my holy name

(Sheherezade)

—I will not tell you my name.

Even as I will not tell you where I am going.

I have done enough for Earth. Earth will likely hate me for liberating it anyway. Liberators are usually despised.

In the stars, I see my future. As I see it in the eyes of my son.

"Robin?"

"Mommy?"

"Tell me a story, will you kid? Mommy's tired."

"Okay Mommy."

He looks more like Hamid than me, I think. He has the widest eyes. His voice reminds me of Aamina.

"Once upon a time in the land of the stars, an old man came to visit. And he was very tired because he'd come such a long way. And the people in the stars didn't know his name or who he was, they hadn't seen him before. But they gave him water to drink and asteroids to eat because he was an old man and they knew he'd come a long way."

I curl my feet up into the cushions, as Robin stares out of the ship, into tinted darkness, as Foo plots his course.

"And this old man looked a lot like Daddy, with a big beard, and big brown eyes, and like Daddy he didn't say a whole lot, he just looked at you, and you felt like you knew what he was saying. And that old man, he left a dog behind, a big black dog, and the old man left. And the people in the land of the stars didn't know where he went. But they wished that they did. They loved that dog forever. It was the best dog they'd ever seen. It was bigger than a house. And it howled into the sky with light from its mouth."

I close my eyes.

"Was that a good story Mommy?"

"Yes it was."

I am a daughter of the sky and I am going home—

ABOUT THE AUTHOR

Robin Wyatt Dunn writes and teaches in Los Angeles. He was born in Wyoming in the Carter Administration. You can find him online at www.robindunn.com.